GHOST SCHOOL

By Robin Wasserman

Illustrated by Duendes del Sur

Hello Reader — Level 1

ISBN 0-439-44227-3

Designed by Maria Stasavage
Printed in the U.S.A.

It was a dark and stormy day.
 , , and went to visit

a friend.

 and stayed in the .

They could not play outside.

They were bored.

There was nothing to watch on .

There were no to read.

There were no more to eat.

There was nothing left to do.

"Like, I'm bored, ," said .

"What should we do now?"

 did not know.

But had an idea.

"Let's go to !" he said. "We can visit our friend Mr. Rines."

Mr. Rines was a teacher at the .

They left a for , , and . Then and went to .

But something was wrong. The was *very* dark and *very* empty.

"Where are all the students? Where are all the teachers?" asked . "Maybe a took them!"

"A ? Ruh-roh!" said .

"Like, let's go, . We have to find them!" said.

and looked everywhere.

They looked inside every .

They looked under every .

 found a and a piece of

 .

 found an .

But they did not find the students

or the teachers or the .

They went to the music room.

It was *very* dark and *very* empty.

They looked everywhere.

 found a .

 found a 🎺 .

But they did not find the students

or the teachers or the 👻 .

They followed Scooby's to the

lunchroom.

But the lunchroom was *very* dark

and *very* empty.

They looked everywhere.

 looked under every .

 looked on top of every .

But they did not find the students

or the teachers or the .

and left the lunchroom.

 found a .

It was a closet . The closet was *very* dark, but it was not empty.

 found a .

 found a .

They did not find the students or the teachers.

But they did find a !

"Run!" cried .

 and 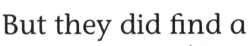 ran out of the closet.

They ran past the lunchroom.

They ran past the music room.

They ran out of the .

They ran right into , ,

and .

" !" cried .

"Jinkies!" said . "A ? Where?"

 and showed them the dark and empty  .

Then and showed them the 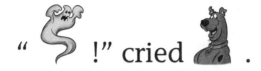 .

"That's no 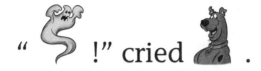 ," said 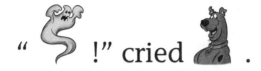 .

"Look, this is just a mop and a sheet!"

"If there is no , then where are all the students?" asked .

"Where are all the teachers?"

"The students and teachers are safe at home," said .

"How do you know?" asked .

 , and smiled.

Then all together they said,

"Because today is Saturday!"

Did you spot all the picture clues in this Scooby-Doo mystery?

Each picture clue is on a flash card. Ask a grown-up to cut out the flash cards. Then try reading the words on the back of the cards. The pictures will be your clue.

Reading is fun with Scooby-Doo!

Fred	Scooby
Velma	Daphne
Shaggy	Scooby Snacks

television	house
school	books
ghost	note

chair	desk
paper	pencil
drum	apple

nose	trumpet
table	door
broom	bucket